Hey Jasmine!
Let's Go to the Park

by
Amber Nichole

Illustrations by
Mike Motz

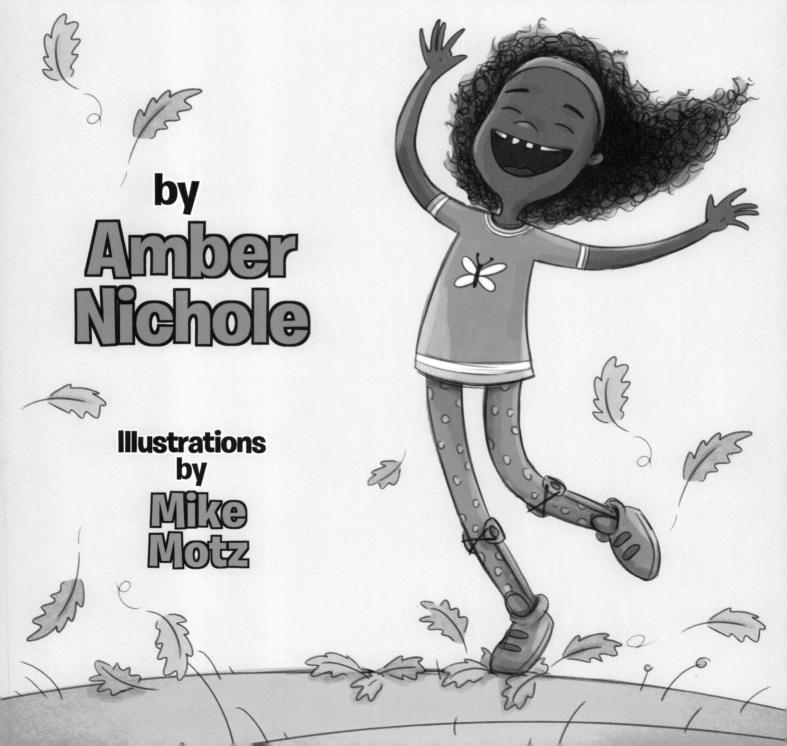

Dedicated to my beautiful Jasmine.
Your spirit, determination,
and love of life is so inspiring.
I love you so much!

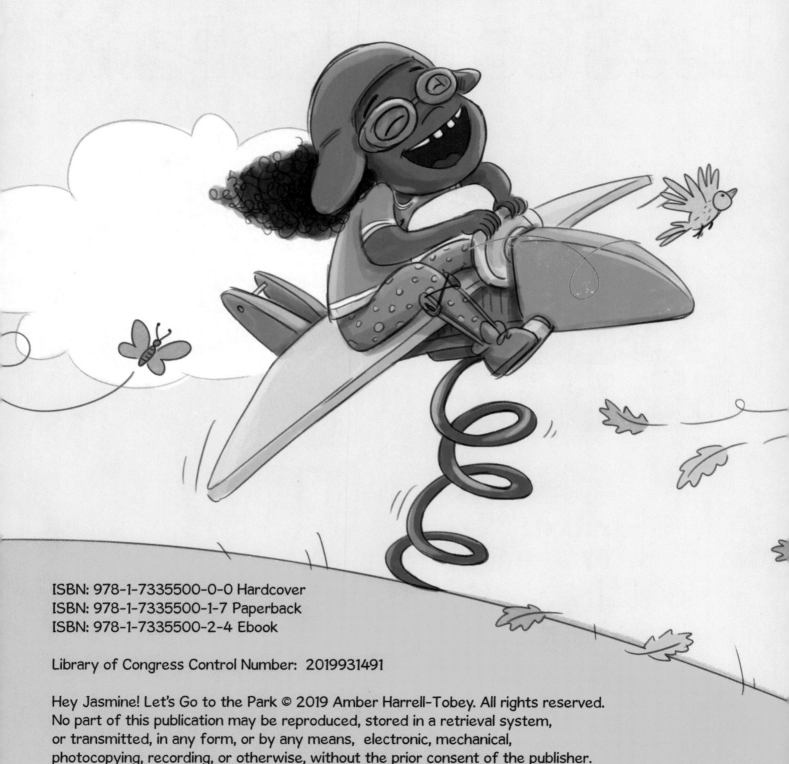

ISBN: 978-1-7335500-0-0 Hardcover
ISBN: 978-1-7335500-1-7 Paperback
ISBN: 978-1-7335500-2-4 Ebook

Library of Congress Control Number: 2019931491

Hey Jasmine!
Let's Go to the Park

One day, Jasmine and her mom were driving in the car.
"Hey, Jasmine! Let's go to the park," said Jasmine's mom.

"Whoo hoo!" screamed Jasmine.
Jasmine was so excited to play with the other kids.

Jasmine and her mom arrived to see all of the kids having so much fun. Jasmine ran as fast as she could to the playground.

When Jasmine asked if she could play with different kids, none of the kids would play with her. They pointed at her drool. They laughed at her leg braces. They called her a monster and ran away.

This made Jasmine really sad. Jasmine has cerebral palsy, which makes it hard for her to control the muscles in her body.

Her mom gave her a hug and told her, "Some kids have to learn how to play with other kids who look differently than them. I know that mean words hurt your feelings. I am sure you will find someone nice to play with."

Just then, a little girl came to Jasmine and asked, "What are those?" as she pointed toward Jasmine's legs.

"My braces," said Jasmine.

"Why does she have to wear those?" the little girl asked Jasmine's mom.

"Jasmine walks on her tippy toes. The braces help give her muscles a break. Walking on your tippy toes can be very painful after a while," explained Jasmine's mom.

"My name is Kemeyah. Do you want to play with me?" said the little girl.

"Sure. Let's go!" replied Jasmine.

Kemeyah had never seen braces on someone's legs before, and she was curious to see if Jasmine could do the same things she could. "Can you play with your braces on?" asked Kemeyah.

"Yes," replied Jasmine.

The girls ran to the playground.

"Hey! This looks like a mountain," said Kemeyah. "Watch me. I can climb all the way to the top. Can you?"

"Sure. Look at me," said Jasmine as she reached the top.

"Let's climb on the blocks and pretend we are on the moon. We can pretend your braces are rockets with turbo speed," suggested Kemeyah.

"Let's go!" screamed Jasmine with excitement.

"5, 4, 3, 2, 1. Blast off!" the girls yelled.

The girls were having so much fun. They flew high on the swings like birds in the sky. They made bird noises and flapped their wings.

Up and down they went on the seesaw.
They pretended to be bunny rabbits as
they laughed and screamed with glee.

Back and forth they flew on the plane as they pretended to be pilots.

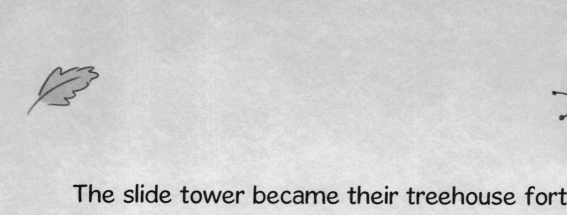

The slide tower became their treehouse fort. They swished down the slide over and over again. Jasmine's braces didn't stop her from doing anything.

Jasmine was so excited that she began to drool more than she had before.

"Why does she do that?" asked Kemeyah.

"The muscles in her mouth are stiff and it makes it hard for her to close her mouth. She can't help it. I have to remind her to swallow and carry a tissue to help her wipe," Jasmine's mom replied.

"What do you want to go on next?" Kemeyah asked Jasmine.

"The monkey bars. They are my favorite!" Jasmine replied.

"We can be superheroes and save the day," said Kemeyah.

"Daddy, I need help," called out Kemeyah as she reached for each bar.

Jasmine's mom stayed close by when it was Jasmine's turn. "Step back," Jasmine said as she motioned for her mom to move back. Jasmine didn't want any help.

"I can do it all by myself," she was excited to say. Jasmine swung from bar to bar with such speed and ease. Kemeyah gave Jasmine a high five when she was done.

Jasmine and Kemeyah were having so much fun,
but it was now time to go home.

"Thank you for playing with me, Kemeyah," Jasmine said.

"Yes, thank you for being so kind. You made Jasmine have a great time today," Jasmine's mom added.

"You are welcome. I had fun too," replied Kemeyah.

"See you next time," said Jasmine as she and her mom waved goodbye and walked away.

Meet
Amber Nichole

Amber Nichole is a mom and an educator who has a passion to help others. Her daughter, Jasmine, was born with cerebral palsy. Jasmine inspires her to create books that educate others about special needs kids.

CPSIA information can be obtained
at www.ICGtesting.com
Printed in the USA
BVHW021340140719
553408BV00002B/2/P